Pascal & Monty

PASCAL POODLE PERSEVERES

Written by Kirsty Lavin
Illustrated by Glen Holman

PASCAL POODLE PERSEVERES

Meet Pascal, a poodle, with black curly hair,
who spends every day asleep on his chair.

At least that's what his family all seem to believe
(Sally, Samantha, Sonny and Steve).

When in actual fact, as
they all leave the house,

Pascal calls his sidekick,
Montgomery Mouse.

The pair meet at their office
in a horse chestnut tree

where they work all day long
and drink cups of tea.

Pascal and Monty (as he's known to his pals)

run a great business called '**SAVE THE ANIMALS**'.

I want to tell you a story I will always remember,
it was a cool autumn day at the start of November.

A hare hopped in through the big bark door.
"I'm Hattie," she said as she shook Pascal's paw.
Hattie explained why she was there,
Pascal took notes and listened with care.

"So, this morning," said Hattie, "when I went for a jog
I heard a voice shouting 'HELP'
through the pea-souper fog.

I followed the cry and guess who I found?

My friend Robbie Robin trapped in the ground.

The poor robin was sobbing. He looked totally stuck.

He's been there for hours in that brown, gloopy muck.

I tried my hardest to save him,"
Hattie continued her tale,

"I reached and I leaned, but each time was a fail...

...Robbie told me to find the mouse and the dog,

he needs to be rescued from the big, stinky bog.

So that's why I'm here, can you help me, please?

By the time I left Robbie the mud was up to his knees!"

"Let's go!" announced Pascal and without any delay,

he grabbed his red scarf and set off on his way.

They sped down the street and into the wood

where they found the poor robin;
half feathers, half mud.

"Oh, Pascal," said Robbie, "am I glad to see you!

Help me, I'm stuck! What shall I do?"

"Don't worry," replied Pascal, "I have no doubt

that with effort and teamwork we'll soon get you out."

Robbie was out of reach, the floor was a muddy mess,

how could they all make this mission a success?

Monty searched up high, Pascal sniffed on the ground,
then they looked at the wonderful things they had found.

Leaves shades of orange, yellow and red,

thorny conkers, four pumpkins
(each one shaped like a head).

"Hmm," pondered Pascal, "this could be tough."

He thought for a minute, then let out a loud **WOOF**.

"I've got it! Let's make a long, leafy string,
we'll throw it around Robbie and pull him out with a PING!"

Hattie watched as they used the leaves to make
a colourful rope as long as a snake.

They then lassoed the robin as quick as they could,
they refused to be beat by this puddle of mud!
The pair pulled together with a heave and a ho,
neither Pascal nor Monty would ever let go.

They tugged with such force, Robbie lifted a bit,
it all looked so hopeful until the leafy rope split.
"Oh no," Monty cried, "we need a new plan,
we need to save Robbie as fast as we can."

Pascal picked up a pumpkin,
"Let's make a stepping stone trail.

We can do this, we've got this! This plan cannot fail."

The pumpkins were heavy and tricky to budge,
it took teamwork to lift them across the swamp sludge.

As Monty secured the final pumpkin in place,
a worried expression crept over his face.
The bright orange boulders were vanishing fast,
"They're sinking," he yelled, "this path will not last!"

Plan B hadn't worked, what would they do next?

The animals all looked a little perplexed.

With time running out, Robbie made a loud shriek

as the mud began to creep up to his beak.

"Come on, we can do this. We will never give up.

We've got this, keep going!" encouraged the pup.

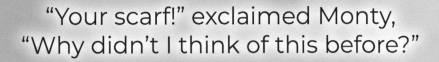

"Your scarf!" exclaimed Monty,
"Why didn't I think of this before?"

Pascal looked confused and scratched
his head with his paw.

Monty quickly explained his idea to his boss
about how they should make a scarf bridge to cross.

Pascal, Monty and Hattie all worked as a team
to turn the red scarf into a balancing beam.

When each scarf end was secured to a tree
Hattie bounced across to set her friend free.

Robbie happily hopped to the end of the bridge,

they celebrated his freedom
with a group hug and a squidge.

"Thank you so much!" Robbie chirped so gratefully,

"Now if you'll all excuse me,
I need a bath and a cup of tea!"

Hattie and Robbie then headed for home,
leaving Pascal and Monty in the wood all alone.

The poodle looked at his pal
with a knowing glint in his eye.

"It's amazing what you can achieve
when you persevere and really try!"

Monty showed he agreed with a proud, friendly grin,

they then strolled back in the sunset
to where this story did begin.

They tidied the office, Pascal locked the big bark door,

SAVE
THE
IMALS

ready for any adventure tomorrow may have in store.

Back home (just in the nick of time),
Monty went straight off to bed.

Pascal laid on his mat, waiting to be fed.

The family gave their pet some food
and a toy to play with too.

I don't think they have a clue
what he's been up to today, do you?

THE END

Printed in Poland
by Amazon Fulfillment
Poland Sp. z o.o., Wrocław

12603259R00016